Home Grown

Joe Mannherz

A Jake Rivers Adventure
#2

Books by Joe Mannherz

All For Nothing

Copyright 2022 by Joe Mannherz

Published by Mannherz Music LLC

All rights reserved.

Library of Congress Cataloguing-in-Publication date available

ISBN: 979-8-9876703-1-6

This book is a work of fiction. Names, characters, places, and incidents are either the product of the author's imagination or are used fictitiously, and any resemblance to actual persons, living or dead, business establishments, events, or locales is entirely coincidental.

Table of Contents

For all the nonbelievers

Chapter 1
In Tune

He didn't know why he was so nervous. It's not as though he never played in front of a live audience before. True, it was the first time his band would be playing in public since their breakup many years ago. But still. He was going to chalk it up to what every performer experiences prior to a stage performance, i.e., the jitters, and work through it, just as he had hundreds of times in the past. But his hands felt a little unsure, and his mind a little unsteady. If it wasn't for his manager, Mike Lipsky, and his dogged determination and relentless persistence in reorganizing the band, this performance would never be taking place at all. He was grateful to Mike, but he realized that although he should be feeling happier, at the moment, he wasn't. This fact he acknowledged to himself, understandably so, since the group's disbandment several years ago was not under the most congenial of circumstances. And many of those issues had yet to be resolved. But putting all that aside, he was glad for the chance to play together again, and prayed, that this time, things would work out differently between them. He hoped. The determined knocking at the door brought him out of his brief reverie.

"15 minutes to curtain," sounded a robust male voice from beyond the dressing room door.

"Thanks 15," he responded, in the standard theatrical vernacular.

He reached over the arm of the couch and grabbed his 6-stringed acoustic Martin. He loved this guitar. It was given to him by his parents many years ago. He wrote most of his music on it, but never had a chance to play it on stage until tonight. It's not as though he never wanted to, but the band in general was labeled "a rock group," due to the style of songs they performed, and the instruments utilized to back up the title. He never thought in the past that using it would be apropos to their 'style,' so he never bothered bringing up the possibility. Not until now. It was his only concession asked for, regarding tonight's performance. And he was slightly surprised, as well as grateful, that his manager and band members had acquiesced. As a matter of fact, Mike thought it was a great idea to show off the band's versatility.

"We're trying to appeal to as many people in the audience as possible during one performance," Mike claimed during one of their rehearsal sessions, and to his surprise, everyone agreed. This was going to give him the opportunity to play one of his favored ballads that he wrote for his girlfriend, 'Penny'. Unfortunately, Penny would never get a chance to hear it. This made the playing of it, for her, even more poignant.

"10 minutes to curtain" sounded the now familiar voice of the stagehand.

"Thanks 10," he replied.

After applying the 'auto-tuner' to the neck of his guitar, he began the slow but necessary turning of the guitar's machine heads, in order to adequately stretch the strings to produce their correct intonation. He had to chuckle to himself when he thought about how easy it was nowadays to perform this task, as opposed to bygone days when you had to use a tuning fork, or your ear only, to achieve this goal. Now, all you had to do was look at its digital readout, and this simple machine would tell you precisely when you had achieved each string's 'perfect pitch.' *"What will they think of next,"* he thought to himself. *"If only the tuning of someone's character or personality was this easy, there would be less conflict in the world. And in my life,"* he reflected. *"Maybe that invention would be the next big breakthrough,"* he wished.

Finger picking his way through the introduction of the song, which was his preferred performance style, and would be tonight for this particular ballad, he mentally acknowledged that the guitar was tuned to his liking.

"5 minutes to curtain," announced the stagehand.

"Thanks 5," he said as he gently placed the guitar in its case and secured its clasps. Standing up from the couch on which he was sitting, he turned to look at himself in the wall-to-wall mirrors that were situated over his makeup table and surrounded by lights. Pausing, while instinctively reaching for a comb, he realized that this, him, was as good as it was going to get. He put down the comb, picked up his guitar, walked across the room, and opened the door just as his manager, Mike, was about to knock.

"Oh geez!" they said in unison, while ducking out of each other's way.

"Maybe that's what I need," he said to Mike, "a good old rap in the head."

"Why?" asked Mike. "Anything wrong?"

"Just a little preshow jitter, that's all," he admitted.

"Hey, there's nothing to worry about, you guys sound great. Even better than you did in the past," claimed Mike.

"Thanks," he said to Mike.

"Break a leg," Mike intoned, in the theater's usual expression of 'good luck.' He would have shaken Mike's hand at this statement, but he realized he was carrying his guitar in his right hand. They therefore acknowledged each other with this generation's version of affirmation; the head nod.

While walking up the steps and through the backstage area, he hoped that Mike was right. He made his way downstage and into the wings just behind the front curtain. From this position, he had an unobstructed view of the entire stage without being exposed to the audience. This was one of his favorite places, and moments in the theater. You could see the audience, but they couldn't see you. You were <u>on</u> the stage, but didn't have any responsibilities, yet. The perfect location at which to meditate.

He wouldn't have had any trouble meditating about the forthcoming show if it wasn't for his upset stomach. He thought by this time, it would have gotten better. He reluctantly had to admit to himself, that it was actually getting worse. And on top of that, he was beginning to feel lightheaded, and his hands were sweating.

"Oh great," he said to himself, *"that's all I need right now. Maybe I <u>should</u> have let Mike hit me in the head."*

Chapter 2
Business as Usual

"Good morning, good morning," I robustly said to the ether after opening my office door, and taking several long strides into its interior. There, to my surprise, in the office's reception area was not only Doris, my secretary, but Ms. Rose from across the street. Ms. Rose, this city's professed Greek gossip and 'busy body,' never leaves her first-floor apartment where she lives. I've never seen her anywhere else but on her veranda across the street, but low and behold, 'surprise,' here she was. Prognosticating that her intimate conversation with my secretary had 'come to a conclusion,' she lifted herself off the corner of Doris's desk, while patting her hand, saying, "thanks for nothing, dear," and started to leave. Before I could get the 'what-the-hell-are-you-doing-here' expression off my face, Ms. Rose intoned,

"I just can't believe Mrs. Handratty was sleeping with the banker's brother-in-law." I gave Doris a, *'you-weren't-supposed-to-tell-anybody,'* stern look, when Ms. Rose smacked me on the arm as she walked by, saying,

"She didn't tell me anything, Jake. But you, you on the other hand, play a lousy game of poker. Thanks for the confirmation, Jake. Remind me to invite you over to our poker night on Tuesdays," she exclaimed, while waving goodbye over her shoulder, as she sauntered her way triumphantly across the street. While hanging my head in utter dejection, I said out loud, to myself,

"You would think I'd know better by now."

"You'd think?" commented Doris, as she handed me my morning's mail, while trying to hide the large smirk on her face. Before I could chastise her for the smirk, she asked me,

"And. How are my favorite nieces doing this morning?"

I can smell a segue when I hear it.

My 3-year-old twin girls have no biological relationship with my secretary, Doris. But you wouldn't know it from their interactions. Even before they were born, Doris was at my wife Nina's 'beck and call.' After the birth, we could hardly get her out of the house. I was going to start charging her rent, but knowing Doris, she would probably just ask for an increase in salary. So, we let her stay. She was not only wanted, but welcome, all the way around, and seven times over. She doesn't reside with us physically, but you would never know it. It was bad enough that I didn't know what to do without her at the office, but now, I don't know what to do without her in my life. Period. And Nina feels the same way.

I walked over to Doris's desk, and positioned my right buttock in the space that Ms. Rose had just vacated. I leaned toward her in a confidential manner. Recognizing my change in demeanor, Doris rolled her office chair over to where I was sitting, placed both elbows on the desk, and her chin in her hands, and with a benevolent glow on her face, smiled, because she realized that storytelling was about to commence.

"The other day," I began, that's my equivalent to '*Once Upon a time,*' "Nina and I were in the kitchen preparing breakfast. The girls walked in with their heads together, intoning in hushed whispers, what a 3-year-olds equivalent would be, I'm only surmising here, of how they would 'save the world' and not get caught in the process. After satisfactorily concluding their conversation, while standing in the middle of the hallway, they shouted in tandem,

"Barney! Barney!"

Recognizing his name, as all good well trained Bernese Mountain dogs should, he came galloping, and I don't use that term loosely, through the house up to the girls. Upon reaching them, before he could lick them to death, they both shouted, "Sit!"

He immediately did so. With satisfied expressions on their faces, they abruptly turned their backs to each other, and in an exact reproduction of a good old fashioned western 'high-noon-shootout', they preceded to walk apart from each other to opposite ends of the house. I don't know how they enacted this scene with such precision, because we normally don't watch that much TV in the house, and especially refrain from shows with violence." This thought gave me pause to consider another viable option. I looked at Doris, and just before I could ask her if she was the culprit, she exclaimed,

"Don't Look at <u>ME</u>!"

Without tangible evidence, I let it drop, and chalked it up to a mystery. Mystery or not, "Nina and I were transfixed with astonishment. After reaching their predetermined destinations, some 50 feet apart, the girls turned and faced each other. They then preceded, in a respectively alternating cadence, to command the dog to "Come." Then "Stay." "Come." "Stay."

The poor dog, in answer to each demand, would start to move, then stop, then move, then stop. Speaking on the dog's behalf, I can't imagine what the poor thing must think of, when he sees them standing side by side, normally. He's either concerned about his double vision, or writes it off as another doggy hallucination. He now had to look at them respectively when they spoke, because he had to turn his head 180 degrees, which means he <u>could</u> only see them 'one at a time'. And he saw the same person alternate commands, to his utter bewilderment, and his conflicting sense of 'master's satisfaction'. This went on for at least a minute, until mental exhaustion overcame the poor dog and he decided just to lie down where he was, and closed his eyes figuring, 'this position couldn't possibly offend anybody.' I couldn't decide, at this moment in time, whether my daughters were savant prodigies, or the spawn of the devil himself. I slowly turned on my stool and looked at my wife, whose tears were flowing freely from her eyes while shaking her head side to side and covering her mouth with her hands."

It was at this point in the narration of the story, while laughing uncontrollably, that Doris had to excuse herself before she urinated on her office chair. As she was running for the bathroom, I said to her,

"But I'm not finished."

To this she just stammered,

"Stop! Stop!" and kept on running.

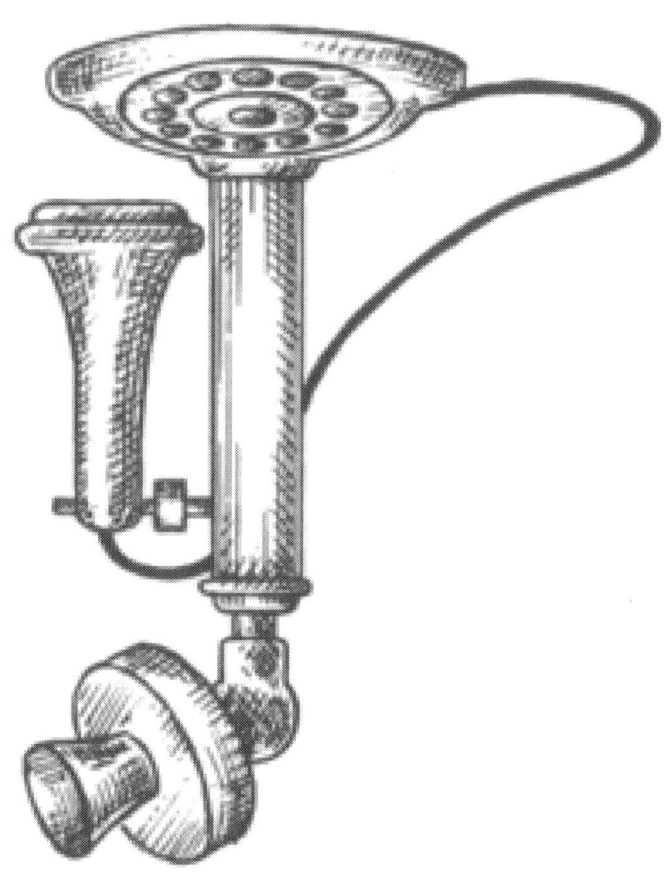

Chapter 3
Business, not so usual

By the time Doris emerged from the bathroom, I had read half of my morning mail while seated at her desk. She took one look at me, and broke out in hysterical laughter while running back into the bathroom. At least she had the good sense to shut the door. It didn't obliterate the wailing completely, but it was tolerable from the reception area. I sat in poignant reverie of 'the morning in question,' realizing that both I, and my wife, had just witnessed a future memory, together. While smiling, I stood and ambulated toward the bathroom to make sure Doris wasn't going to hurt herself. While in the process, the front door to the office opened, and in walked detective Murphy of the Baltimore Police Department.

'Murph' and I go back a long way. He was my mentor and instructor when I first joined the force, and he was the first officer to endorse my endeavors in becoming a private investigator.

Patrick 'Murph' Murphy was a legend in this city, and a hero to me. I do have to say, regrettably, that the years were beginning to take their toll on poor Murph. In his mid to late 50s, he was starting to show some gray around the temples, some girth around the abdomen, and a decidedly slower gait than he did, what appears to me, say, 'yesterday.' He was still sharp as nails though, and you could read about him making 'collars' on a regular basis throughout the city.

"HEEEYYY," we said to each other in unison as we wide-stepped 'Conan' style toward each other. Upon contact, we naturally gave each other a 'man-bear-hug' with more,

"HEEEYYY's," as we patted each other on the back. He then surprised me by lifting me off the floor while in his embrace.

My opinion of his 'fitness level' went up a few notches. As we broke our embrace, in order to view each other at arm's length, Murph said to me, while scouring,

"You don't look so hot."

Never letting a compliment go to waste, I replied,

"Have you looked in a mirror lately, yourself?"

After giving each other the 'evil eye' for a few seconds, I broke eye contact first, while chuckling,

"What brings you out of your hole, you old fox?"

"Don't I even get a chance to say 'hi' to Doris, and ask about the twins?" he inquired, looking stupefied.

"Not today, I'm afraid," I answered, while glancing quickly towards the bathroom.

"We ran out of coffee this morning, and we were just about to go out and get some. Why don't you rest your tired feet, and you can tell me what you're doing here. And, we can enjoy that cup of coffee later. By the way, what <u>ARE</u> you doing here?"

At this remark, his expression grew troubled.

"Let's go into your office and we can talk" he said.

Once again, I recognized a segue when I heard it. As I led him towards my inner office, there could be heard a soft murmur coming from behind the bathroom door, which naturally, caught Murph's attention.

"What's that noise?" he inquired.

"Oh, that's just Doris. She's in the bathroom, you know . . 'Woman stuff, 'I whispered.

To this, he just nodded in affirmation.

Cruising passed my inner office door, which I was holding for him, he took a second to say 'hi' to Babe.

Babe is an 8-ft, 6-in Indian cobra who resides in my inner office. I'm not, by any means, one who you would call a "reptile person." I'm more of a Bernese Mountain dog kind of guy. But the snake was given to me by an affluent Indian client I worked for some time ago as partial payment for helping him settle a family inheritance dispute. His financial payment was more than adequate to cover my services, but he felt "obligated" to extend his gratitude by giving to me one of his pet cobras. It's a member of a rare variety of one of the only non-poisonous cobras still in existence in India. Who was I to say "no?" And, as it turned out, the snake is great company. It doesn't talk much, and agrees with everything I have to say. It keeps all my clients civil during our discussions, and the office free of rodents in her spare time.

Murph and Babe are 'old buds.' After a knuckle wrap on her aquarium tank, Murph just waved his hand and said,

"Hey, Babe."

"Hey, Murph," Babe hissed in reply. She then retreated to the sanctuary of her aquarium tank to continue doing whatever cobras do in the middle of the day. Murph pulled up a chair to my office desk and sat, as I did the same with mine.

"Tell me what you know about Jeff Raines," Murph asked.

"Oh boy," I exclaimed, "I haven't heard that name for a while." I leaned back in my chair, crossed my hands over my middle, and stared up at the ceiling collecting my thoughts.

"Good guitar player, great songwriter. His band, 'Rapture,' used to record at my brother's studio, and I used to help mix the tracks. So, I got to know all the members of the band. Let's see, Tim Gentry, drummer. Great meter and good chops, slightly narcissistic. Bob Rhodes, bass guitarist. Great hand speed. I hear he had some gambling issues, the ponies I believe. Ben Timmons, piano. 'Tiny,' they used to call him. He was so tall he'd have to sit down to play the piano, and they still had to boost the piano. Good backup singer. I hear he's got a couple of drug busts on his rap sheet. The band was doing really well for a couple of years, and then there was that incident during their Oakland tour when Jeff's girlfriend, Penny, committed suicide. Things started to deteriorate after that for the band, and they eventually broke up. Haven't heard much about any of them since. I hear they're supposed to get the band back together again for a so-called 'reunion tour' that's supposed to take place soon. That's about it. Why do you ask?"

Doris's voice resounding over the intercom interrupted our conversation by asking,

"Coffee's on, can I get you boys a cup?" I looked at Murph who nodded his head.

"Yeah Doris, that would be great, thanks."

I leaned back in my chair, and gave Murph my undivided attention.

"They did get the band back together again, and the concert took place last night." As he said this, he slid a newspaper across the desk towards me and flipped it open. The headlines read,

Jeff Raines Perishes on Stage.

"Holy cow!" I exclaimed, while picking up the paper.

"What's the skinny? Anything so far?" I asked.

"No, nothing yet," Murph said. "We are treating this case as suspicious however, because he didn't have any pertinent past medical history to explain his sudden demise, that we know of, so far. He's being autopsied as we speak."

"Could you keep me in the loop on this Murph, I'm curious."

"I can do better than that," said Murph. "That's why I'm here. With all the 'defund the police' movements taking place nowadays, we're a little short-staffed downtown in the investigative department. The brass knows of your previous connection with this group of people, and would like to know, if this turns out to be more than just a plain old heart attack, would you be interested in doing some behind the scenes sleuthing for us? Compensated, naturally."

"Murph," I reproachingly said, looking somewhat unappreciated. "You know you don't even have to ask me twice. As a matter of fact, you didn't even have to ask me the first time."

During our handshake that transpired across my desk, Doris brought in the coffee. After all the informal salutations were addressed, and the coffee poured, Doris excused herself and began to leave. Before she could get past Murph, he reached towards her and lightly touched her forearm, stopping her, saying,

"I hope you feel better."

To this statement, she gave me a very puzzled look, as she made her way out of the office. I just responded by shrugging my shoulders and raising my eyebrows in complete bewilderment of Murph's last statement.

Chapter 4
When it Raines, it Pours

When the front door opened, and my twin daughters in tandem verbally intoned, 'Dee-Dee', 'Dee-Dee', I knew Doris had arrived. I was hoping that the twin's current habit of turning every single word into a bi-syllabic phrase was just a phase. In their defense however, they do here Nina referred to me as 'Dad-dy', and I to her as 'Mommy', not to mention our Bernese Mountain Dog as 'Barney.' So, it was no real surprise that when I referred to Doris as D, which I do frequently, she thus became to the twins, 'DD'. To extrapolate on this theme, when the twins are in my office, they refer to the cobra as 'Babe-bee'.

See what I mean?

Aunt Doris was here today to babysit the girls, which she does approximately twice a week, to allow mommy and daddy to have some 'one-on-one' adult interaction, if you catch my drift. Babysitting our twin girls has become Doris's second most favorite pastime.

Babysitting ME is her first.

Thank God.

"Coffee for everybody?" Nina asked, which was followed by raised hands from all the adults in the room.

After the death of her father four years ago in Russia, Nina decided to immigrate to the United States to be with me. Go figure.

She still maintains her associate professorship (honorary) at the M.V. Lomomosov State University in Russia, as well as her Diamantaire status with the department of the interior, but she can now claim the same status here at the University of Maryland, and with the Museum of Natural history in Washington DC. On a part-time basis, that is. Looking after the twins takes precedence. She has also applied to become a naturalized citizen of the United States. I couldn't be prouder of her.

"Anybody home?" came a familiar booming voice through the front screened door, accompanied by the sound of simultaneous knuckle wraps.

"Come on in, Murph," I replied, which was then followed by the traditional Rivers household greeting. The girls, in tandem, started to chant "Mur-phy , Mur-phy" while proceeding to envelope each of his shin bones while sitting on a foot respectively. Barney, not to be left out, decided to leap up and place his paws on Murphy's shoulders while licking his chin. This tableau, and the chanting, continued as Murph made his way down the hallway into the kitchen; girls astride each leg, and the dog back-pedaling.

"Looks like the gangs all here," Murph said.

"Barney, down!" I commanded.

"Girls!" Nina chided.

"I got this," exclaimed Doris, as she gathered up and herded both the girls, and the dog, into the adjacent family room.

"Never a dull moment," I exclaimed to Murph, while handing him a cup of coffee.

"And take your eyes off my wife. You know I'm the jealous type."

Both he and Nina simultaneously blushed while casting their eyes downwards. I always knew Murph had a sentimental attachment towards my wife, and I teased him about it every chance I could. He told me once that she reminded him of his childhood sweetheart.

"To what do we owe the pleasure of your visit, Murph?" Nina asked. "Business or pleasure."

"You know it's always a pleasure being here, but today, I have to admit, there is a little bit of business to be thrown in as well," he stated, while straddling a kitchen stool across the island from where I was sitting.

"We just received the medical examiner's report on Jeff Raines. He was poisoned. Thallium." Nina and I exchanged concerned looks, as we both sat down our coffee mugs in order to concentrate on what Murph was telling us.

"They are a little stymied at present, because while confident about the etiology, they can't determine the source. It wasn't ingested, because they didn't find any traces in his stomach or inhaled for that matter, ditto for the lungs. And they didn't find any puncture wounds."

This was all intriguing to say the least. And, as if reading my mind, Murph continued,

"And, there were no trace substances in the eyes from the possible use of eye drops. CSI has gone over every inch of the dressing rooms and stage areas, as well as his house, and so far, they've come up with zilch."

"And will this 'zilch' help them to find out who did it?" asked Nina.

It took Murph and I a few seconds to process what Nina had just asked.

"No, Hon, I explained. 'Zilch' isn't a person or a thing, it means zero. Nothing. They haven't found a thing yet."

"Oh!" she exclaimed in embarrassed understanding, while continuing to reorganize the kitchen after breakfast. Murph and I just smiled at each other as he continued:

"We've taken preliminary statements from everyone in the band, including their manager and the stage crew, as to their best recollection of where everyone was that evening, and what transpired within a twenty-four-hour period of his death. We're going to keep the investigation going on our part to uncover the nitty gritty, but we thought we'd give you the green light to go sleuthing into anything, or anyone you thought pertinent to the investigation."

"OK," I said in response. "Send copies of all that information you just told me about over to my office, and I'll go through it. I'll probably have a chat with everyone involved first and foremost, and I'll keep you abreast of anything I find out."

"Can do," he said. "Now, what's for lunch?"

Chapter 5

Home field advantage

I go over to my brother's recording studio as much as time will allow. There's not as much of it now as it used to be, time that is, because I have Nina and the girls to take care of, as well as devoting most of it to my primary duties as a private investigator. I still call it my "brother's" studio, because he was the originator of, an inspiration for its existence, and the driving force behind its success. After he passed away, he bequeathed the studio to me. I do like to be involved in the creative recording and mixing of music, but unfortunately, not as much now, as I mentioned, as in the past. I've tried to hire competent engineers to carry on in my brother's stead, who I feel confident will uphold his traditions, i.e., attention to detail, collaborative intervention, honest pricing, and reliable resources, which were his trademarks. Many of the clients we still serve today have been with us for years. This is where I first met Jeff Raines and his 'Rapture' band members, and I thought it a good idea that from here, I should conduct my interviews with each one of them individually. Using the studio as my 'home field advantage' to give them a sense of "familiarity," in order to gain their trust and confidence, and hopefully honest answers to my questions that would be forthcoming. And if that strategy didn't work, there was always Babe.

"If you want to win the game," my dad always said, *"use every advantage you have."*

I gathered up all the information that Murph sent me, along with all of my own personal knowledge of the band members individually and collectively, and started to formulate my plan of action. We were starting with known associates first, because as history has taught us, most acts of violence, i.e., murder, rape, kidnapping, domestic abuse, etcetera, are committed by family members, close relatives, or associates of the victim. If that aspect and focus of our investigation didn't 'bear fruit,' we were going to be left with a very large subset to have to work with, i.e., the general population. *"One step at a time Jake,"* I told myself. *"One step at a time."*

People, being who we are, are not perfect. We all have problems. And depending on how we handle said problems either gives us Peace of Mind, and allows us to live within our own skins, and become respected by our fellow human beings, or we become pariahs unto ourselves, devouring ourselves from within, or acquiesce to our own evil and therefore become shunned from society like lepers. Marriages succeed or fail depending on the attitude, personality, and conviction of only two people. In this situation, we're dealing with a band that has five plus members, all with their own personalities, convictions, likes and dislikes, temperaments, attitudes, and <u>problems</u>. I thought it best to take the path of least resistance, and start my quest for the truth in an order of ascending difficulty, and that meant getting in touch first with the band's general manager, Mike Lipsky.

He wasn't that hard to find. Like most professional businessmen, they're usually found at their office. I gave his secretary my name when I called, and asked if I could speak with Mike, directly. She put me on hold for a couple of seconds, and then Mike picked up the phone.

"Jake, how the hell are you?"

"Pretty good, Mike. How about yourself?"

"Not bad, uh, . . . considering."

"Yeah, I hear 'ya."

"Pat Murphy said you would be giving me a call. So, I guess this is it, huh? What did they do, twist your arm, or threaten to pull your license if you didn't come back on the job?" asked Mike.

"Neither," I chuckled. "They just knew that we had history, and they thought the third degree coming from a friend in a familiar environment, would be a lot easier to swallow then in a cold spartan room, surrounded by floodlights."

"Anything to write home about to date?" Mike asked.

"Not yet, Mike, I'm just getting started, and you're number one on my hit parade."

"I guess I should feel flattered then," he chided.

"You should Mike. You organized and held the band together back in the old days, and God knows what you did to have them bury the hatchets and get back together again. To that, I can only guess. Or should I say, you can fill in the blanks when we get together for our chat."

"And when and where are we having this clandestine meeting?" asked Mike.

I let the obvious metaphoric innuendo slide, and said, "How about tomorrow morning, 9:00 o'clock at the studio?"

After checking with his secretary, Mike said that wouldn't be a problem.

"Do you want me to give you directions, or should I send somebody over to pick you up?" I said to lighten the mood.

"You wise ass," he inferred. "That's why I always preferred working with your brother. {silence} "I sure do miss him."

"You and me both," I managed to say.

"Why is it Jake, that all the good ones lead the way?"

I didn't know what to say to this. I knew from the onset, in suggesting we meet at the studio, that it was going to be difficult confronting past acquaintances over the current situation, much less knowing the spirit of my brother was going to oversee the proceedings.

"Have the medical people finished with Jeff yet?" Mike asked.

"I'll fill you in with all the details when I see you tomorrow. Still take your coffee black?" I asked.

"Sure do," he said. "And make sure it's hot."

After hanging up, I double checked all the telephone numbers I had for the rest of the band members, because it was imperative to have my initial meeting with all of them tomorrow. To ensure this occurred, I divvied up the list, and gave half to Doris, then instructed her to cancel all scheduled recording sessions that were in the books for tomorrow. After hearing Mike's last comment, I realized that the public, to date, had no idea that Jeff Raines had been murdered. Tomorrow's interviews should be interesting.

Chapter 6

The Manager: Mike Lipsky

Good managers are always early for meetings; comes with the territory. That's why I wasn't surprised to see Mike walk through the back door of the studio 10 minutes early. He stood for a few seconds with his hands on his hips, surveying the interior, as though being welcomed back home by a friend. In his late 50s to early 60s, he looks like everyone's favorite uncle. He always reminded me of JK Simmons, the actor who played in the farmers insurance commercials.

"Would you look at this place," he declared. "It doesn't look much different than it did when I was here last, and neither do you," he said, while walking and extending his arm towards me in greeting. We clasped hands in the center of the room.

"Good to see you Mike," I said, "come on in and have a seat. The coffee's hot and black as usual." I led Mike into the inner sanctum of the studio itself where we took seats in front of the 96-channel mixing console. From this vantage point, you had an almost 180-degree panoramic view through soundproof glass into four independent, soundproof recording rooms. We affectionately called this room, the 'Hub.' I could tell, from his nostalgic expression, that the view, and its past significance, was not lost to Mike.

"My God Jake, the music we made here." And in the ensuing silence, it could still be heard.

"I hear you got married," he said, breaking our reverie.

"And have two daughters," I proudly announced.

"Holy Shit. Time does fly, doesn't it?"

"Speaking of time, Mike, I don't want to rush you, but I don't have a lot of it today. I'm interviewing every band member later, after you." That statement elicited a surprised response from Mike.

"So, I'm going to glean from them, individually, their own perspective as to how they fit in with the band. What I need from you, is to give me the 'overview' from their manager's point of view. In short, what happened?"

Mike leaned back in his chair, crossed his legs, and gripped his coffee mug while saying,

"You know most of them. You've met them before, so I'll make the history brief. Jeff Raines, guitar player and probably the most levelheaded member of the group. Bob Rhodes, bass guitarist, part time gambler. He used to bet on ponies even when he was in high school. It got a little out of hand while the band was together, and he accrued a lot of debt which unfortunately he couldn't pay back. I know this because I caught him embezzling funds from the bands bank account. Jeff knew it too. But he didn't know I knew. And he didn't know I knew, he knew."

At this point in the summary, Mike looked at me with an expression of 'Hey, I was their manager, that was my job, what did he expect?' and I acknowledged his expression. "I know Jeff had a talk with Bob because I saw the money slowly begin to rematerialize back into the band's asset fund. But to this day, I don't think it was ever fully repaid. Ben 'Tiny' Timmons, pianist, drug, and ETOH abuser. Not to the point where it ever affected his playing or singing ability, to my knowledge. But I know the mere presence of 'substances' elicited an undercurrent of tension among the band members themselves. He had a couple drug busts while the band was together, but it never affected the other band members personally or the band's performances, schedules, or monetarily for that matter. And then there's Tim Gentry, drummer, narcissistic prick." He stopped then, and put his fingers to his lips and said to the ghost of my brother,

"Did I just say that out loud?"

"What a personality. I don't think he liked or was liked by anybody. It's a good thing he was a fabulous drummer, or nobody would have associated with him. He just pissed everybody off. Oh, and I almost forgot, Penny. Rachel 'Penny' Coin, Jeff's girlfriend. Probably one of the finer things that ever happened to Jeff. Nice girl. Used to travel everywhere with the band. Nobody seemed to mind. Damn shame what happened to her. While the band was touring out in Oakland, Penny found out that her mother had died from cancer back east and it tore the poor girl up inside. A few days later, she committed suicide.

"Now you take all of the above, put it in one big 'human' kettle, turn up the heat, stir and cook for four years, and that's basically what the band was made of."

"And what about the reunion, the comeback? How did you pull that off?" I asked.

"I just gave it 'time.' Time for the fire to go out, and the soup to cool down, and hoped that what transpired in the past could be forgiven. Then crossed my fingers and prayed the 'soup' was still edible. When I broached the subject with everyone, I was as surprised as they were, when everyone agreed. And it sure did look like we were heading in the right direction."

"And what about the night of the performance?" I queried.

"Electric. Everyone was ecstatic. Couldn't ask for a better venue. We all had our own separate dressing rooms, and everybody was in good spirits. I stopped by Jeff's dressing room just as the band was collecting itself together to go on stage. He said he felt a little nervous, and his stomach was upset, you know, 'preshow jitters.' But, other than that, he said he was looking forward to the performance. We all gathered in the wings, as was our usual preshow rallying point, bid each other good luck and started the show. I watched the show from my usual perch in the wings. Everything went according to plan for at least three quarters of the first half. Then, it was time for Jeff to perform his solo. He picked up his acoustic guitar, sat center stage and began to play the ballad that he wrote for

Penny. He got halfway through the ballad, and . . . and keeled over," he stammered. "End of story."

I couldn't think of how else to tell him, so I just told him.

"Mike, the medical examiner's report came back the other day, and it showed that Jeff was poisoned. He was murdered."

I now know how a military chaplain feels when he must tell a parent that his or her child was just killed in combat. The profound look of horror, shock and remorse warring over the same facial expression was heart wrenching. I rolled my chair forward so that I could place my hands on his knees, in a show of empathy, while he hung his head in his hands and stammered,

"Oh God, Oh God."

"Mike. Mike," I repeated, in an earnest attempt to gain his attention, and help divert his emotional state and frame of mind into a positive realm. He finally acknowledged my presence, and need of his attention, so I therefore continued.

"Mike, I need you to keep this information under wraps. No one but the medical examiner, the police, myself, and now you, know this fact. And I need it to stay that way for at least another 24 hours. Do you understand?" I asked him. He nodded in affirmation while wiping his eyes with the back of his hand.

I escorted him out of the building and to his car, because I wanted to make sure that he was physically and emotionally capable of driving home. When he assured me that he could, and I believed him, we shook hands and parted company, wishing each other well, and promising each other we would keep the lines of communication between us open.

As I watched Mike drive away, I would bet my professional investigator's license on the fact that I had just witnessed an honest, truthful, and innocent emotional reaction to a hitherto unknown catastrophe. I, therefore, had no qualms with myself, whatsoever, in writing Mike off my hit list.

Chapter 7

And then there were three

I heard Bob Rhodes arrive at the studio before I saw him. He was always partial to Harley Softails, and apparently, old habits are hard to break. He strolled in through the back door clad in black chaps, helmet and jacket, and sporting a full black beard. He looked like someone right out of an Errol Flynn pirate movie. And not one of the good guys. He saw me through the glass enclosure, and I waved to him to come back. I met him at the entrance to the 'Hub' where we shook hands.

"Bob, how have you been?" I asked.

"Pretty good, Jake. You look well," he inquired.

"Couldn't feel better," I told him. "Thanks for making the time to come over today."

"Hey, anything to help the troops. You know, once a band member, always a band member. Oh, by the way, I want to tell you how sorry I was to hear about your brother's passing. I meant to get in contact with you then, but it was for the same reason that I didn't attend the funeral. I was out of town that week. As a matter of fact, I was out of the country, and I didn't even know about it until I got back a couple weeks later."

"Thanks Bob, I appreciate that," I said.

"He sure knew how to work this baby," he commented, as he laid his hands upon the multimixer. "Not that <u>you</u> didn't know what you were doing," he chuckled, "but your brother just had . . . 'the touch.'"

"You don't have to tell me. He taught me everything I know. And then some." We strolled over to the chairs where I offered him a seat.

"Did I ever tell you that he said you were his favorite bass player? "

"You're kidding!" he replied. "The way he used to bitch at me during recording sessions, you would never have known it," he trumpeted.
"That's how love works Bob," I said. "Don't worry about it, he used to bitch at everybody." And we both had a laugh on common ground.

"I don't know how much more I can tell you, than I already told the police. I'm assuming that's why I'm here. To talk about the band?"

"Yes," I answered. "The police are trying to put together a comprehensive picture of what happened that night, as well as acquiring a more in depth and cohesive look at how the band functioned in general, which includes knowing a little bit about their history, and that's why they asked me to help tie things together."

"Hmm, I guess that makes sense. But it sure does seem like a lot of extraneous fuss for a guy who just had a heart attack and died. I guess they have to do that for everybody who's in the spotlight, huh Jake?" he asked.

I was watching him carefully during this last interesting rant for any unusual 'tells' that he may be giving off, subconsciously.

"Yes, I'm sure they do that for <u>everybody</u>, Bob." I replied.

"You and Jeff go back a long way," I enquired, changing the subject. "Weren't you two in a high school band together?"

"Oh yeah, we sure were. That's where we first met. The Chevelles, it's what we called ourselves then, and six months later, we changed it to . . . something else. I don't even remember. We were the same age, and so we had the same classes together for four years. Pretty much."

"Didn't the two of you attend Woodlawn high school in northwest Baltimore? Just down the street from Pimlico racecourse? Isn't that where you acquired your taste for 'the ponies'?" I asked.

He gave me a penetrating leer as he continued by saying, "It's no secret that I love the horses. Loved 'em then; love 'em now. Jeff and I would sneak out during the middle of the day, cut a class or two, bet on some ponies and then make it back to school before anybody knew we were even gone."

"But that didn't last long, in Jeff's case, that is." I remarked.

"No Jake, you're right. Jeff was always the smarter of the two of us, and he realized that if he didn't <u>stay</u> in school, he couldn't learn, and if he couldn't learn, he couldn't make much of himself. Me on the other hand, well, I never did learn that lesson. I did graduate. Jeff saw to that. He was a good friend. Yep, I sure did graduate. A little worse for wear, and maybe with a few less dollars in my pocket, but . . ." and he shrugged his shoulders.

"Rumor has it," I began, "that playing the ponies and managing money during the band years was still a problem of yours, and a source of some contention between you and Jeff?"

"You heard that did you? Well, I did run into a stretch of some bad luck. And because I wasn't able to pay back the loans in time, I asked Jeff if he would help me out. Like I said, always a good friend. And I <u>was</u> paying him back gradually throughout the years, but somehow, I never could seem to make ends meet. But Jeff knew me, and he didn't seem to mind, much. But he always knew I was good for it. I just never got a chance to pay it all back."

I'll give him this, he did look contrite during this last "bearing of his soul" soliloquy. So, this was the story he was going to be sticking to. OK. I don't have to play all my cards at once either.

"So, tell me about the reunion. When Mike got in touch with you."

"I was over the moon. I can't tell you how happy I was that Mike called me and told me what his plans were. After all, I was never one of the band members who wanted to break up in the first place, just ask Jeff. Oh,

God help me," he said in self-chastisement, as he scanned the room hoping someone else would.

"And the night of the show? Tell me a little about that evening," I asked.

"We really didn't see much of each other that evening because we each had our own private dressing room. The stage was already preset, and pre tuned, so we didn't have to worry about that. We did have our usual ritualistic meeting backstage just prior to going on. Everybody was hyped. Everybody was ready. Talk about going from a super high, to a super low in a matter of just a couple hours. I guess if you have to kick the bucket, that would be the place to do it. Go out doing what you love best. When you think about it, it's kind of fitting, don't you think?"

He looked at me then for some sign of affirmation. I just didn't have any to give him.

"I guess that would be true, if you go out on your own terms," I said. To this he looked puzzled.

"What do you mean?" he asked.

"The coroner's report came back a little while ago," I began in explanation. "It indicated that Jeff was poisoned. He was murdered."

Envision if you will, a slow, smoldering tea kettle coming to boil, attempting to launch itself off the stove it was sitting on, while simultaneously holding on so as not to leave the earth. This was the vision I was now confronting, and I knew it couldn't last. And it didn't. It got worse. When the chair could not confine him any longer, he threw himself out of it, took it, and threw it across the room into the filing cabinets. He then began to punch the cabinets to death with his fists while simultaneously shouting,

"NO! NO! NO! NO!"

I had to physically restrain him from hurting himself any further. A true and pure visceral gut reaction if I ever saw one. I knew questioning or prodding him in this, his current state, was going to do neither one of us any good, so I focused all my energies on returning Bob to some semblance of a human being. It's a good thing I had the foresight to schedule these consecutive meetings several hours apart, because it took quite a while for Bob to regain, and retain, a calm demeanor. And even longer for him to stop re-inquiring as to the accuracy of the medical examiner's report, then its authenticity, then their conclusions, until he appeared to accept what I had initially told him to be true. I knew he couldn't drive his bike back home because his hands were in rough shape, and I knew they needed medical attention. I called him a cab, and instructed the driver to take him to the Johns Hopkins outpatient clinic. I then asked the driver if he would be so kind as to inform me when he had indeed delivered Mr. Rhodes into their care. I said goodbye to Bob, and told him I would be calling him soon. I returned to the studio to straighten up the damage, assess what I had just observed, then waited for Mr. Timmons to arrive.

Chapter 8

Two for the Road

"Hey Jake!"

"Jesus!" I shouted, jumping about a foot out of my chair.

"You scared the crap out of me. Do you always sneak up on people like that?" I panted, while catching my breath.

"I don't mean to, it's an old habit," explained Ben 'Tiny' Timmons as he ducked his head under the door lentil to enter the hub. "Maid's day off?" he asked, surveying the room.

"Yep."

"Is that Bob's bike out back?" he inquired, pointing his thumb over his shoulder towards the back door.

"Yep."

"Bob's blood?" he deduced, surveying the filing cabinets.

"Yep."

"Anything you need to forewarn me about before I take a seat?" he implored.

"Nope."

"Could have fooled me." he said, as we both sat down in opposite studio chairs.

"Bob took some information I needed to tell him, a little too much, to heart," I confessed.

"That's Bob," Tiny said. "Bad news?" he asked.

"Yep."

"Bad <u>band</u> news?" he asked again after swallowing hard and rearranging his position in his seat.

"Talk to me about Penny, Ben. Were <u>you</u>, her supplier?"

Both his head and eyes dropped towards the floor as his fingers began nervously feeling themselves, and his body began minuscule undulations 'to and fro' where he was sitting.

"It wasn't like that, Jake. Penny was a great kid. She really was. She was great company for Jeff, and acted as a 'diffuser' for the band in general during our road trips. Everybody loved Penny, Jake. Sure, there were parties, great parties. But never out of control parties. A few drinks here, a few drinks there, just to take the edge off, you know, unwind from the concerts. Never any hard stuff. Mike saw to that, and Jeff saw to that. Hell, I was even on board with that too, if you believe that. I personally wasn't doing much in our heyday, honest, because I knew I would catch so much flack, and I didn't want to be the one to screw up the good thing that we had going."

He glanced over at me at this time to see if his spontaneous confession was in line with what I wanted to hear. I did my best imitation of the 'good father confessor,' and indicated that he should continue 'purging his soul.'

"She came to me one night, about a month before we played in Oakland, all bent out of shape and crying. She told me that she just received word that her mother had been diagnosed with stage IV pancreatic cancer and they only gave her a few weeks to live. She was beside herself, Jake. She didn't know what to do. She wanted to go back home to be with her mother, but that would require money for airfare, and when she got back home, she didn't know if she would have the heart to leave. And then again, she wanted to stay here with Jeff. She said she couldn't eat, and she couldn't sleep, and she came to me because she wanted to know if I had something that would at least let her calm down and rest. I told her that I did, and I only gave her a few sedatives to get by on. Then she thanked me and left. Unfortunately, that same scenario played out again every other night for about two to three weeks. I don't know if she was the type of person who avoided conflicts in general, or she was just in denial about her mother, in the hopes that, if she waited long enough, her mother would somehow survive this current illness. All I know, is the more she remained undecided, the worse her conundrum. As we approached the Oakland concert, that was basically the end of our tour date, I guess she figured we were all going to be flying home anyhow, so she would just wait and go back with everyone. Fate didn't see it that way however, because her mother passed away while we were en route. Penny didn't receive word until we arrived in Oakland. I truly, truly believe to this day, that if Jeff would have been there, none of <u>this</u> (and he indicated the entire world) would have happened."

"What do you mean, '<u>if</u> Jeff would have been there?' Wasn't he with the band?" I inquired, perplexed.

"He was, up until we boarded the plane to Oakland," Ben admitted. "Mike had arranged for Jeff to give a lecture at a songwriter's seminar that was being held at Golden State university in San Francisco, his old alma mater, during the same time interim we were appearing in Oakland. It was easier, and cheaper, for Jeff to fly straight into San Francisco from Reno, where we currently were, and then join us in Oakland for the concert, than it was to go with the group and then detour to San Francisco and then back again to Oakland."

As he was explaining all of this 'virgin information' to me, he had risen from his chair, and began pacing around the studio becoming more animated and agitated in the telling.

"I'm convinced, I'm absolutely convinced, that if Jeff would have been there, none of this would have happened. "

Each "<u>convinced</u>" was punctuated by a fist thumping on the top of the file cabinets.

"If that cock-sucker would have kept his dick in his pants, we, . . ."

In the aftermath of the expletives, there was deathly silence. Ben, slowly rotating his head to look down my line of sight, simply read my expression of, "I beg your pardon, SAY WHAT?" engraved on my face, before he let the air he was holding out of his lungs.

"shit;……. sHiT;…….. SHIT!"

As we say in the 'investigative' world: "the feline has left the enclosure. And none of the King's horses, and none of the King's men, is gonna' put Kitty back in, again." I knew it, and <u>he</u> knew it.

"You want to take a seat Tiny?" I gently said to Ben. "I think it's going to be easier on my filing cabinets, and on <u>you</u> if you did." Acknowledging the wisdom in my suggestion, Ben migrated back over to his chair and dropped.

"Is this what happened with Bob?" Tiny asked.

"How about, you finish the rest of <u>your</u> story, and then we can discuss Bob," I said in response.

He nodded, then took a deep breath.

"The night that Penny found out that her mother died, she was inconsolable. None of us at the time knew, because the information came straight into the hotel and directly to her room. She was in there crying and breaking furniture, for God knows how long, before the hotel management started to get complaints from the other hotel guests about, "the noise." As fate would have it, the hotel management, acquiring the location of the offending room and its occupant from the complaints being registered, discovered in their reservation logs that the room was booked as a group. They weren't getting any direct satisfaction trying to phone Penny, because she wouldn't answer the telephone. So, they called one of us. We may have all registered as a group, but they didn't 'Locate' us as a group. Our rooms were scattered all over the hotel. That's why none of us knew what was happening. None, but the one the hotel management called that night. Oh! I'm sure he had all the good intentions in the world to resolve the situation. And I'm sure, he empathized with her wholeheartedly, as he was trying to calm her down. And I'm positive, that he felt holding her while she was crying was the right thing to do to alleviate her fears. And I'll bet my immortal soul, that there must have come a time, when he put all those well-meaning intentions aside and reverted to the lowest base form of humanity possible, in order to take a band member's girlfriend to bed."

"Oh my God," I cried. "No wonder the shit hit the fan."

"Oh no Jake! The shit didn't hit the fan, then. The shit hit the fan when Jeff found them in bed together."

"He left his conference early, because a couple of the keynote speakers at the seminar failed to show, so everyone had an early dismissal. So, he drove into Oakland, only to be confronted with this scenario. The next two days in the hotel was like a demented, sadistic Chinese fire drill, with the girlfriend, the manager, and all the band members trying to either avoid each other or kill each other. It didn't subside until they found Penney's lifeless body."

"I didn't mean to kill her Jake, I swear, I didn't mean to kill her."

"Wait!" I shouted, while standing up and pacing around the studio holding my own head, because it couldn't absorb any more information. I was on sensory overload.

Ben, in the meanwhile, had physically collapsed onto the mixing board, sobbing, and moaning inconsolably.

All I wanted to do at this moment was hug and kiss my wife and little girls. I think I was in survival mode, and I wanted to get off this emotional merry-go-round. But I realized, after thinking it through, that my emotional survival could wait, others could not.

I regained my seat, and rolled my chair over to Bens.

"Ben. Ben," I implored, trying to gain his attention. He finally recognized me as I clasped his face between my hands, and while our foreheads were only inches apart, looking him straight in the eyes I asked him,

"Ben, what do you mean you killed her?"

Collecting himself, he said that following the investigation by the police, it was determined that Penny had overdosed.

"I know the jury of my peers in the band could have jumped to the first logical conclusion of where the drugs came from, but they didn't. Whether that was because they didn't have it in themselves to give up a band member or they realized I didn't have it in me to kill anyone. I don't know. All I know, is that nobody ratted me out. I had a sneaking suspicion, but I had to be sure. When all the investigation had quieted down, we were still in the Oakland hotel, because none of us were allowed to leave the city until the officials told us we could depart. So, when the situation allowed itself, I went into my hotel room, uncovered my stash, and confirmed my suspicions.

A lot of my inventory was missing, and the rest disheveled. She must have been more observant than I gave her credit for during the times that she was here, asking me for help. I didn't realize, until it was too late, that Penny knew exactly where I was keeping my stuff. Don't ask me how she got into my hotel room, or when. At this point, does it make any difference?"

"I killed her Jake. As sure as if I had force fed the drugs to her myself, she's dead because of me."

While looking him straight in the eye and patting his cheek, I said to him, "Penny may be dead for a lot of reasons, but Ben, you're not one of them. Come on, let's get you out of here."

We stood, entwined in each other's embrace, and shuffled our way through the studio and out to the parking lot. I couldn't think of any logical or rational reason I should tell him about Jeff's demise under the current circumstances. I was done here. I had more people to interview, and more fish to fry than the current person I held in my arms.

Chapter 9

One hit wonder

As if the mere thought of interviewing other people could bring the concept to fruition, a car started to pull into the rear parking lot of the studio. As the day was waning into evening, and the sun was setting just behind the approaching car, I couldn't make out exactly who was driving. But because I knew there was only one band member left, that took the fun out of guessing. The blistering rhythmic percussion and volume of the music that was blaring out of the approaching car left me concerned about whether the person driving was either deaf, or deaf. I continued to help Ben into his car as the approaching vehicle came to a screeching halt about three feet away,
just missing Bob's bike by inches. As abruptly as the car came to a stop, so did its music.

"Boobbyy's . . here," came a rhythmic sing song intonation from a voice exiting the car, "and hey, Jake Rivers, long time no see and wait, is that Tiny? Tiny, how's it going man?" came the litany of greetings from the man emerging from the vehicle. Upon seeing Tim Gentry exit his car, Ben began to extricate himself from the seat which I just positioned him in, attempting to come through the window of the door I just closed behind me.

"Tim, why don't you go into the studio and have yourself a cup of coffee while I say goodbye to Ben. I'll be with you in a minute."

"OK. Good to see ya' Ben. 'Bobby', 'Bobby,' Tim called to his band mate, he apparently believed was in the studio, as he made his way through the back door. Stooping, so that I could get a better look at Ben, in order to assess his current state, he appeared crestfallen.

"You OK to drive, Ben?" I asked him through the car's open window.

"Yeah, I'm good." He replied.

As I stood and began to turn to head into the studio, Ben stopped me by placing his hand on top of mine, i.e., the one remaining on the window's ledge.

"Thanks Jake, you do your brother proud." he intoned.

"Go home and get some rest, Ben, I'll be in touch."

I remained stationary for a moment to watch, as Ben started his car and drifted his way slowly out of the parking lot.

"Lives that are touched by other lives who in turn touch others. 'Six degrees of separation.'" I was always fascinated by this concept. I was reflecting on this as I begrudgingly turned and started walking across the parking lot to the rear door of the studio. I reminded myself that as a private investigator, I had to remain neutral and objective during any investigation, i.e., take information as it presents itself. You may not like the box it's wrapped in, or who it is

that's delivering it to you. It's simply your job to do the research, collect, collate, and disseminate the information, and let it tell you what the conclusion is. With that objective in mind, I entered the studio.

"Where are you hiding Bobby?" Tim asked me as I came into the hub. With his feet up on the console sipping his coffee he looked like he owned the place.

"He left a little while ago," I remarked, "and get your feet down." While complying, begrudgingly, he inquired,

"So, this is where the third degree takes place?"

"Is that what you think's going on?" I asked.

"Well, judging from the look of the place, the absence of Bobby, but the presence of his bike, and the condition of poor Ben just a little while ago, I'd say I was on the right track."

"I do have some questions about the band that I'd like to ask you; some loose ends that need tying up."

"I figured as much, go ahead, shoot," he said, while leaning back in his chair and putting his feet back up on the console. After several seconds of my best 'Private Eye stare' he put his feet back down.

"Tell me about your relationship with Penny."

"Oh, I figured that cat was out of the bag. Well, we didn't have a relationship. It was only that one night. One stupid, fucking, night. I was there, she was there, she was susceptible, I was . . .

. . anyhow, it's not like she wasn't willing. And YES, if I had to do it all over again, I wouldn't have gone down to her damn room in the first place. Who'd have known it was gonna' cause all this shit?"

"Do you think Jeff knew how you felt?" I inquired.

"I should hope so. We had enough rows over it to convince Congress. I just wish the two of them could have made-up before she, . . . Oh well."

"This may come as a shock, I hate to tell you, but Jeff wasn't a Boy Scout you know. But you wouldn't know it, would you. Not by the way people treated him. Jeff, the great songwriter. Jeff, the great guitarist. They treated him like he was a Saint. Saint Jeff. The only problem with being canonized while you're still alive, is that you start believing that shit about yourself. Then you have to live up to your own Press. Charity concerts here, pro bono music seminars there, bringing strays in off the street."

The puzzled expression I gave him, after he uttered this last sentence, must have convinced him I didn't know quite what he was referring to, when he said,

"Oh, come on Jake, you remember, the roadie. The kid who used to hang out at our rehearsal halls, and at your studio here during sessions; the pimply faced kid that used to go fetch us coffee?"

Now that he mentioned this, I do recall seeing someone hanging around them during their recording sessions. I gave him a look that said, 'don't let me stop you now, you're on a roll.'

"Ray Pierce. The 'kid.' Groupie that used to hang outside the back door of our practice sessions. During the colder months, we had to let him in or watch him freeze to death outside. A real pain in the butt. He was always underfoot and in the way. 'Can I do this? Can I get that? What's this for? How does that work?' To keep him relatively satiated, Jeff started to teach him how to play the guitar. I do have to admit, the kid wasn't bad, and he learned fast. But then I had to go and open up my big mouth."

Once again, I gave him my best, "I'm listening" expression.

"I mean, it got to the point where the kid was attending more band rehearsals than the actual band members themselves. I said out loud one day, basically just bitch-kidding, 'my God, why don't we just give him a job?' And wouldn't you know it, Mike overheard it and thought that was a good idea, so he hired the kid as our permanent roadie. He would set up all our instruments at the gigs. Tune the guitars, set the spotlights, and still fetch coffee."

"And you found this to be a problem, because?" I asked.

"Like I initially said, 'Saint Jeff.' He was just wallowing in his own good intentions. It was kind of sickening to watch."

"This is all fascinating information, but let's get back to the band," I said.

"I assume, since you agreed to get back together for this reunion tour, that you and Jeff had buried the hatchet?"

"As best we could. It was like an unspoken truce between us. If **I** didn't bring it up, and **he** didn't bring it up, we were both OK living in the silence."

I had the police report right here with me that attested to where everybody was before, during, and after the performance, and I didn't have much more to ask Tim at the moment, besides, I was tired, so I sat down my coffee cup and stood. Extending my hand, I said,

"Thanks a lot for being forthright with me, Tim, I appreciate it. Thanks for helping tie some of those loose ends." And we shook hands.

"Now what are we gonna' do?" he asked.

"What's going to happen now?"

"What do you want to happen, Tim?" I asked.

"I want the band back," he said.

Chapter 10

Home, the Hunter

I snuck into the house through the back door. Because the hour was late, I didn't want to wake anybody up, in case they had fallen asleep. As I walked by the family room, the television was on full throttle. Reminded me a little of Tim's car. There, in the corner of the couch in front of the television sat Doris. Or should I say, 'reclined Aunt Doris,' with her head back, eyes closed, and completely gone to the world. On each shoulder, just as entombed as their babysitter in the depths of slumber, reclined my twin daughters. And at Aunt Doris's feet, or should I say, in the supporting role of her footstool, was Barney, awash in doggy dreams. I knew Nina was about, because I could hear her shuffling through the kitchen. With her hands in the sink, and her back facing me, I shuffled towards her in the hopes of catching her unaware. Just as I was enveloping her waist from behind, she murmured,

"Just because you're a private investigator, doesn't give you the right to sneak up on people. Long day?" she asked.

"Have I told you how much I love you?" I whispered in her ear.

"Not that I recall, today," she complained.

"But you can start," she purred.

"I've loved you since you walked into that little cafe on Calvert St, and you crossed over to my side of the pond."

She leaned back into me then, and put both her warm soapy hands on mine.

"I've missed you," I said, nibbling on her neck. As we both held each other, I could feel an increase of pressure against my left lower extremity, as well as both feet. As I glanced down, I wasn't surprised to see Barney leaning up against my leg, and our two girls entwined around both of my ankles.

"I see you have everything under control," said Doris from behind us, "so I'll just see myself out, and catch you in the morning."

"Hmm," was all I said in retort. "Drive carefully, see you at the office," I intoned as I heard the front door close.

"Murph was here today," Nina hummed into my chest. "He said he had some information about the case for you, and if he didn't catch you home today, because he knew exactly where you were all day, he'd see you bright and early at the office tomorrow."

"Hmm, not tonight," I said in reply as I stooped down and grabbed each girl respectively in my arms while encircling my wife in the center.

"Everybody's with me tonight," I told them.

Chapter 11

Keep your Sunnyside up

Feeling completely reenergized this morning from the glorious restful sleep I got last night, not to mention all the hugs and kisses I received this morning before I left the house, I bounded my way down the street towards my office without a care in the world until:

"Somebody got lucky last night, huh Jake?" declared Ms. Rose, as she slurped her morning coffee. Not to be deterred by this unwanted interruption, I replied,

"You bet your ass, and it was fantastic. You want me to give you a little demonstration?" I said, as I came to an abrupt halt, and started to climb up the terrace to her veranda; Tongue hanging out of the corner of my mouth and panting hard.

"Help, Police, I'm being victimized by a sex fiend," she yelled into the air while beating me off the veranda with her newspaper.

"That's what I thought, all bark and no foreplay," I teased.

"You better get down before I tell your wife, "she chided.

"You don't have to, she knows I'm great at foreplay, not to mention . . . "

"Help, Police!" she interrupted again while laughing and beating, and laughing and beating at the air, as I quickly withdrew and held up my hands in defeat, while skipping across the street in anticipation of my day. Entering the office, still skipping, Doris was already there, naturally, doing 'Doris stuff.' I skipped across to her, wrapped her in a bear hug while lifting her off the floor, and planted a wet smack, right in the middle of her lips. Dropping her unceremoniously back to the floor, she staggered back, and said without bothering to gain her balance,

"Well, somebody got lucky last night."

"Why is it, everybody says that to me, I don't understand."

Her eyes dilated, and she was just about to explain the 'birds and the bees' to me, when I silenced her with a stern look while pointing my finger right at her and said, "Eh."

We exchanged knowing smiles, and she informed me that the coffee was hot, and that Murph had called and said if he didn't beat you into the office this morning, he'd be right behind you. I thanked her, picked up my morning mail and went into my inner sanctum. It wasn't much longer after that, the front door opened, and I heard Doris greet Murph to tell him I was in my man cave. Seconds later, Murph came through my sanctuary door with coffee(s) in hand, said 'hi' to Babe, and unceremoniously dropped his carcass in the chair directly across from me.

"Well, looks like somebody got lucky last night," he stated. Doris's hysterical laughter could be heard echoing through our place of employment.

"Not you too," I said to Murph's stunned expression.

"Good morning to you too, grouchy," he said in response. "Forget what I just said."

Doris was now totally out of control.

"Doris," I yelled, "would you mind closing the door. Nobody in here can think with all that racket going on."

She laughingly complied.

"So, what's new by you?" he inquired.

While my mouth was opening to reply, he interrupted,

"Besides that."

I took a deep breath as we, in tandem, lifted our coffee cups and simultaneously slurped, while giving each other the 'evil eye.'

"I hear you had a productive day yesterday," he inquired. "Productive AND long," I responded. "Got a chance to interview everybody in the band, and came away with some interesting tidbits, but you first. Doris said that you had some news concerning the case. I'm assuming it's from the coroner's office?"

"Yeah. Are you ready for this? After a couple days of going over Jeff's body from head to toe, and inside and out, looking for the source of the poison, they finally found it. They located it on the tips of his fingers. All ten of them. In heavy doses."

As we both settled back to let that revelation sink in, I mentally explored all the possibilities which that statement could entail.

"Nobody else was affected. Nobody else got sick. And the crime scene crew didn't find traces of the Thallium any place in the building?" I asked.

Murph just shook his head.

"And he didn't get a manicure that day?" I asked.

"Not that we know of," answered Murph.

"And how about you?" Murph asked.

I went on to summarize my findings from yesterday, and to give him my gut impression, i.e., that Jeff's murder was an honest surprise to most of them, and the ones that I didn't tell, I don't think knew. Sure, there was a lot of drama, in-house squabbling, and bad feelings, but whether the animosity quantified enough to commit murder over, was yet to be seen. I told him I was going to take all day today to analyze my notes and compare it with his, the coroners, the CSI teams, and I'd give him a call later if I came up with anything.

"Good by me," he said, as we stood and shook hands. He then said goodbye to Babe. Before he left the building, I saw him stop by Doris's desk, where the two of them had their heads together, chuckling.

"You better not be talking about me," I yelled.

"A little touchy this morning, are we?" was all that came back in a man's timber, punctuated by female giggles.

Chapter 12

I never saw that one coming

It didn't take long, scrutinizing all the paperwork lying in front of me, to realize that I needed more information. I surmised that I could get the best overall rendering of the circumstances from Mike Lipsky, so I asked Doris to give him a call to see if he had some time today to stop by the office for a chat. It didn't take Doris long to respond, saying she had just talked to Mike, and he'd be over within the hour. To occupy the intervening minutes waiting for Mike, I decided to call home and find out what everybody was doing. The telephone was answered by both daughters and the dog, simultaneously, until my wife intervened to bring a semblance of order to the situation, and a smile to my face.

"Your nickel," she intoned.

"Babette, I don't have time to talk to you right now, can you put my wife Nina on the phone."

"Oui, oui Monsieur, une minute s'il vous plait," she responded. "Girls, it's your father. You'll get a chance to talk in a minute. Let mommy talk to daddy first," which was followed by a chorus of, "Ahhhhhh's."

"Babette said you wanted to talk to me?" She had that 800 'phone for sex' sultry voice going on, and I knew I had to watch my step.

"Just calling to see how my favorite three girls are doing this afternoon."

"Most of us are doing fine," she informed me. "But the two 'younger' of your favorites want to know what "getting lucky" means?"

"I'm going to kill that Murph when I see him," I said to the atmosphere in general.

"Don't blame him, Jake," she chuckled. "He was teasing me at the time, and they overheard. But I thought I'd wait for you to come home to explain it to them. I'm curious to know what it means myself."

"When I come home, I'm going to show my number one favorite girl exactly what it means."

"Promises, promises." she chided.

"Jake," Doris interrupted, "Michael Lipsky is here."

"Gotta' go Hon, see you in a bit."

"Bye," she said sadly, "we'll be waiting."

"Doris, send him in," I requested.

As Mike entered the room, I stood, we shook hands, and I gestured for him to please take a seat.

"Did you get a chance to talk to everybody yesterday?" Mike asked.

"Yeah, and I must admit, it was an enlightening day to say the least. I don't know how you put up with 'all that' Mike. You have the patience of a psychiatrist."

I would say it was more of a 'den mother-confessor' roll if you ask me."

"I bet," said I as we chuckled together. "I got the big and little pictures of how the band in general operated and interacted, and I could see where all the animosity and possible hatred could hide, but I don't think anybody was capable of murder. I haven't told Ben or Tim yet about the coroner's report. I didn't see the necessity at the time, but I'll get around to it. Could you fill me in a little more on the role of Ray Pierce. Someone you failed to mention during our first interview."

"Oh, the kid! He was a young teenager we found hanging around the rehearsal hall. A real groupie. He was pretty tenacious, and wormed his way into the practice sessions by doing odd jobs like fetching coffee, running out to someone's car to get something they forgot, those sorts of things. He actually became pretty handy. Almost like a fifth wheel. Most of the band didn't mind him there except...."

"You wouldn't be talking about Tim in particular, would you?" I asked.

"How did you guess," he responded. "I don't know what it was with Tim. The kid just seemed to rub him the wrong way. He used to tease him about being a 'brown noser.' That sort of thing. But that only lasted up to a certain point."

"What do you mean?" I asked.

"Well, Jeff started to teach the kid how to play the guitar, and after a couple months, he got fairly competent. Tim was teasing him one day, about something only Tim would know, and Jeff took personal offense to it. In defense of Ray, he began listing the kid's accomplishments, and bragging about his work ethic. Jeff even boasted that the kid was good enough to play with the band. Well, as you probably guessed, that got a lot of catcalls from the boys, especially from Tim. Jeff took off his guitar and handed it to Ray. The boy looked dumbfounded, but Jeff insisted. So, Ray put on the guitar. Jeff then looked at the rest of the band and said,

"My opening lick from 'tumbled down' off the second album." He looked up at Tim and said,

"Go ahead ass breath, count it off."

After a couple seconds of 'stare-down,' Tim must have decided this was all going to be amusing, so he counted it off, and lo and behold, the kid played the introduction almost as good as Jeff. The band was stunned. Me too. And the teasing stopped from then on."

"Is that when you put him on the payroll?" I asked.

"Yeah, it was around that time. I don't know exactly, but I figured, if he was going to be around, he might as well get paid for doing what he was already doing. He was with us right up to the end."

"Well, I guess that makes sense. When the tour ended in Oakland, there wasn't much left for him to do since the band broke up," I remarked.

"No, I mean right up to the end, as in the concert last week."

"He was at the concert last week? After all those years?" I asked in confusion.

"Yeah. After the band broke up, I helped him to find a job, and because he was overqualified as a stagehand, he landed a position with the arena where we just performed as their head technician. We were as surprised to see him there during rehearsal week as he was to see us. It was like 'old home' week. We didn't have to worry about a thing. He knew all our routines, and our staging, and our instrument requirements."

Mike's last comment gave me pause to consider.

"Mike," I began, "when the police released all your inventory back to you after CSI finished their investigation, was all your equipment accounted for?"

"I think so," he stated. "I haven't done a specific inventory yet, but no one else in the band has complained about missing anything. Why?" he asked.

"I'm not sure yet," I said. "Would you mind canvassing the group, and doing an in-depth inventory, then get back to me and let me know what you find, if anything?"

"Can do, Jake, I'll get on it right away."

"I appreciate that Mike," I said, as we shook hands, and he left the office. A man on a mission.

I called Murph down at the station, with secondary thoughts of chastising him for teasing my wife, but I didn't bring it up at this time because I had other things to talk to him about.

"Murph," I said, "can you do me a favor, and get a hold of the CSI report that listed all of the band's equipment and instruments that they tested, and returned back to the band?"

"Can do," he exclaimed. "Why for and for what are you looking?" he asked.

"I'm not sure yet, Murph. I'll let you know when I find out myself."

Chapter 13

Imagine

The next morning, I was in my office with Aunt Doris, Barney, and the twins. Nina had stopped by earlier and asked Aunt Doris and I if we wouldn't mind babysitting the crew while she did a couple hours' worth of shopping. Before I could raise any objections to the request, Nina was bidding us farewell and exiting the building. Smart woman.

I was seated behind my desk, pouring over the information I had gathered all week from 'interviews to inventory,' including the now revised and current CSI inventory from Murph, as well as the one from Mike. I still couldn't connect the dots. But I knew it was here, somewhere. As I was ingesting my second cup of coffee while reviewing the files, the twins decided to pay Babe a visit. After standing near the center of the aquarium tank for a few minutes, they started walking to opposite ends of the enclosure. 'Where have I seen this movie before,' I thought to myself. Barney, recognizing the same scene as I was watching, simply stretched out on the floor, put his head down on his paws, and began a very deep throated whine. My gut instinct was sending me a warning. The girls, now residing at opposite ends of the aquarium, began calling the snake; "Ba-by. Ba-by." In response, Babe began to rise overtop her glass enclosure. The girls, now satisfied with the snake's reaction, began teasing the reptile by alternately commanding it to 'come'; 'stay;' 'come;' 'stay.' The snake, apparently wanting to have no part in this play, just raised itself higher, expanded its hood as far as it could go, and hissed at the dog on the floor, as if to say, *"you started this."* The next thing I knew, my twin daughters, now hiding behind my office chair said to me, "Babe doesn't wanna' play."

So now it's <u>Babe</u>? I wonder if fear has anything to do with bisyllabic linguistics? Or lack thereof? Before I could put my theory to the test, Doris announced over the intercom that Mike Lipsky was here. I could see him through the open door, and waved him back into my office. I told the girls to go out and see what Aunt Doris was up to. Mentally, I forced myself from saying, "DD."

"Did you get any coffee?" I asked Mike as he shuffled into the room. In response, he just held up the steaming mug he was carrying with him.

"I brought you a present," he said to me, while handing me a CD case. On the case read, 'rapture: reunion tour.'

"We always record our practice sessions for self-critiquing purposes. It's not as good as what you would do at the studio, but for our purposes, it suffices. I put together a compilation for you of the bands last week of rehearsal. Thought you might enjoy it."

I held it, as though he had just given me a Grammy Award.

"Thanks Mike," I said, as I spun my office chair around, opened the CD case, and slipped the disc into my stereo that resides on my credenza. After a few seconds, the sound of the band enveloped the room. Mike sat down in the chair opposite mine, and we both took a moment to enjoy the music.

"They <u>were</u> good," was the obvious thing I said to Mike.

"You don't think I know," murmured Mike nostalgically. "Have you turned up anything yet?" Mike asked me, while surveying the mountains of paperwork piled on my desk.

"I wish I could say yes. I know it's here; it just hasn't told me 'where,' yet."

As we continued to discuss the unyielding information lying on my desk, the CD behind me changed tracks, and 'Penny's song' began to play. My twin girls, who had wandered back into my office during our conversation, stopped in front of the speakers saying, "pretty daddy." And to that, I had to admit, the girls were 'right on.' Jeff never sounded better while masterfully playing the guitar. While looking at Mike as he reminisced, I couldn't help but mentally recall what he had said to me earlier in the week, about all the 'good ones leaving us first.' And I couldn't help but imagine all the songs that would go unwritten by this talented musician. The music that we, their public, would never get to appreciate. It was all lost.

<u>Lost.</u>

And it was. I sat up straighter in the chair as the concept crystallized.

"That's it Mike. That's what we've been missing. Because it is."

"What are you mumbling about Jake?" Mike inquired, perplexed.

"It's not <u>what's</u> here, it's what's <u>NOT</u> here," I rambled excitedly. "His guitar. His acoustic guitar. Where is it? It's not on the CSI's list of examined items, and it's not on your list of the band's current inventory. It's not here."

"It has to be there," Mike intoned. "He played it that night on stage."

"I know Mike, that's what I'm talking about. It <u>must</u> be here. But it's not. You didn't ship it back to Jeff's condo?"

"Why would I do that Jake, nobody's there."

"Right. You didn't give it to one of the other band members?"

"No."

"Then it has to be at the arena."

"It isn't Jake, I was just there this morning."

"What?" I asked him, surprised.

"That's where I was all morning; at the arena, re-checking our inventory."

"Well, maybe one of the band members recalls packing it up or transporting it that night."

"We didn't pack or transport anything that night, Jake. All <u>that</u> was done for us by the arena crew."

"You said you were there all morning?" To which he nodded.

"Who did you talk to?"

"Ray Pierce."

"Doris!" I shouted. Call the arena, tell them to locate Ray Pierce, and have them detain him there. I'm on my way."

In the process of closing shop i.e., turning off the stereo, grabbing my car keys, I asked Mike,

"What did you guys talk about this morning?"

"I told him about your helping the police with their investigation, and that you had interviewed me and the rest of the band, and that at some point in time, you would probably be getting around to talking to him."

That brought me up short. "You told him that?"

"Yes," he answered.

Doris came into my office at that time saying,

"I just talked to the Arena, and they said that Ray Pierce had just gone home because of illness." Mike and I both exchanged concerned looks.

"Do you know where he lives?" I asked Mike.

"Yeah, he lives in the same apartment building near 'Federal Hill,' in which he always resided," he answered.

I turned to Doris, 'deja vuING all over again,' and said, "Doris, hold the Fort." I then turned and scooped up my twin girls in a big hug, and told them to mind their Aunt Doris.

"Barney, behave!"

As I turned to leave the building, Mike asked,

"Jake, do you mind if I come with you?"

"Hell no, Mike. Who else is going to be the navigator?"

Chapter 14

Elementary my dear Watson

It was only a 15-to-20-minute driving excursion from my office, through downtown, over to the Federal Hill side of the city. We parked directly in front of Ray's building in a designated 'no parking zone.' Private investigator 'tag perks.' As we bounded up the front steps towards the building, Mike checked his records to confirm that Ray Pierce was residing on the second floor, room 210. After opening the front door, we followed each other up the narrow staircase leading to the second floor. Soft guitar music could be heard playing in one of the apartments located on this floor, and as we approached the door to 210, the music got louder, i.e., not recorded music, but live guitar playing. Mike and I both exchanged meaningful glances as he rapped on the door.

"Come on in, it's open," suggested a male voice from within. Mike and I ventured forward into the living area in response to the salutation. There, seated on a couch, was a man in his early 30s playing very calmly and proficiently on an acoustic guitar. And it wasn't any random tune that he was picking, it was Penny's theme.

"Hi, Mr. Lipsky," he said, "nice to see you again. Mr. Rivers, it's nice to see you again as well. You probably don't remember me; it's been a while since we've seen each other."

"I do remember you, Ray," I replied.

"Mr. Lipsky said you might be stopping by to pay me a visit, so I thought I'd wait."

"Wait? Wait for what, Ray?" I asked.

"Wait for you to pay me the visit," he answered.

His nonchalant guitar picking continued during our extended verbal introduction.

"I do have a few questions I would like to get your answers to," I queried.

"Oh, I betcha' there's more than just a few, Mr. Rivers," he chided.

As he continued to play, Mike glanced my way and pantomimed to me, *"that's Jeff's guitar."* After having my initial suspicions confirmed by Mike, I continued.

"Mind if we sit down, Ray?" I asked.

"Oh, by all means, please do, make yourselves comfortable."

"Nice place you have here, Ray," I said as I sat.

"Thanks, Mr. Rivers. I like it. I've been here a long time. Mike helped me afford this place, by giving me a job with the band, years ago. I don't think I ever really properly thanked you Mr. Lipsky. You've helped make my life very comfortable these past few years." he stated.

"You're welcome, Ray," Mike intoned, as we both looked at each other, undecidedly not knowing as to where this conversation was headed.

"Those were the days, weren't they, Mr. Lipsky? Writing new songs, learning how to play together as a real band. I know I didn't count for much back then, but I felt that the menial things and jobs that I was performing was helping the band concentrate on the big picture," he admitted, coughing lightly.

"And we had fun, didn't we, Mr. Lipsky? I know most of the guys appreciated what I was doing. Well, most of them, most of the time. Jeff and I really fooled 'em, didn't we, Mr. Lipsky? When he taught me how to play the guitar, I mean. We sure fooled them. I can still see the looks on their faces when Jeff handed me the guitar to play. And then the completely different looks on their faces when we finished playing. That was pretty great," he said, coughing again.

"It really broke my heart when Penny died, Mr. Lipsky. I guess she was the key to the band's success, huh Mr. Lipsky? Their 'muse' so to speak. Because everything fell apart when she left, didn't it Mr. Lipsky."

Ray's playing was becoming audibly softer and slower, and tangibly more imprecise. And he was starting to slur his words.

"Tell me what happened at the show, Ray," I asked.

"Well, wasn't that a surprise? You could have knocked me over with a feather when I saw the boys walk through the arena door that afternoon like they'd never been apart."
{cough}

But nobody called <u>ME</u>, Mr. Lipsky. Nobody let ME know the band was back together. I thought we were family?"

"We are family, Ray. We are," said Mike.

"Yeah, that's what you say now. {cough}

"But where was I supposed to fit in? You had everybody you needed. I didn't ask for much, just a chance. Jeff said, one day I would have a chance.".…. {cough}

"I think he meant, that you could have your own chance with your own band, Ray," said Mike.

"No! No, he meant with <u>this</u> band. {cough} I would have a chance with this band. But <u>HE,</u> he never came through."

"<u>You,</u> you never came through Mr. Lipsky."

Ray's guitar playing had all but stopped by this time.

"I loved Jeff, Mr. Lipsky. But the only things I knew how to do was make coffee, and play the guitar. And you always said we didn't need two guitar players. What else could I do?"

With this statement, Ray unhanded the guitar which then slid slowly off his lap onto the floor. Mike made an instinctive move to catch the guitar, but I made a faster one to stop Mike before he could touch it.

"Jake?" Mike said imploringly to me.

"It's too late Mike," I said to him, shaking my head.

"I wasn't too bad, was I, Mr. Lipsky? I could have made it, couldn't I?" he asked in almost a whisper, while blinking rapidly, and leaning heavily to one side.

"You <u>were</u> good, Ray. You were <u>really</u> good," choked Mike.

"Sorry.. to put.. you.. through.. all.. this trouble, .. Mr. Rivers," Ray just barely managed to say.

"No trouble at all, Ray," I acknowledged.

"I'll. . say 'hi'. . to . . your brother . . Mark . . for you . . when . . I . . . see 'em."

After this utterance, Ray fell face down onto the floor.

Chapter 15

One less bell to answer

Why does it always rain at funerals? Have you ever noticed that? Or is it my imagination? My mom and dad got married in the rain, and they had a <u>great</u> marriage. Maybe this <u>is</u> a good sign.

I don't know whose idea it was. I haven't made up my mind yet in determining whether it was done for a practical, spiritual, economic, or 'whatever' purpose. Or, there was an element of the macabre in the decision making. But whoever organized two funerals on the same day, in the same cemetery, no more than 50 feet apart, without knowing, or even worse, knowing the history associated with the two individuals, and did it <u>anyway</u>, needs some serious psychiatric counseling. To say it was "uncomfortable," was putting it mildly. Because basically, all those 'gathered together' knew each other, and we all knew why we were here. It was just bizarre to alternately visit the grave sites of victim and perpetrator without feeling slightly, 'uneasy.' Even that's too mild an expression. "Guilty?" I guess that would all depend on 'which side of the aisle you're sitting on.' Isn't that what they say at weddings?

I decided to bring the girls to the funeral to keep my wife company, and Doris busy. I knew they were a little too young to understand any of this, but I thought it would be good education for them. And besides, they're intelligent girls and well behaved. They may not understand "what's going on," but they sure are sensitive to the fact that if everyone else is solemn and quiet, they need to be as well. And they were. I know when I get home, there'll be at least 1000 questions as to what all this pertained to. I wasn't really looking forward to that. I just might defer all those questions to my intelligent wife, who keeps reminding me that 'she is', all the time.

It was nice to see all the band members in solidarity. It's sad to think that it takes a tragedy for that to transpire. The scuttlebutt had it, during the wake, that Mike was exploring getting a new guitar player, and keeping the band alive. I would gauge the atmosphere surrounding the surviving band members to be 'positive' in nature to that suggestion.

CSI and the medical examiner conjointly confirmed that the Thallium found on Jeff's fingers was identical to that found all over his guitar strings. It didn't take a rocket scientist to extrapolate how it got there.

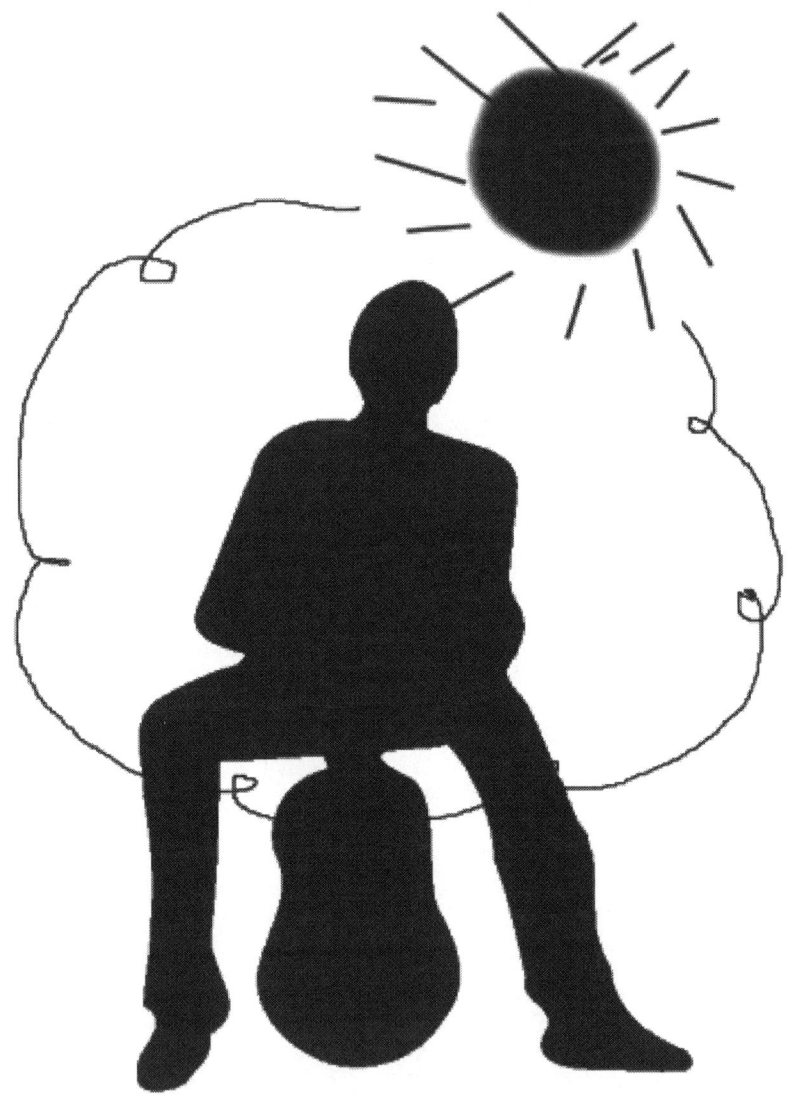

Epilogue

Once in a while, the spirit of my brother moves me, and I have a good idea. I attribute the good ideas to my brother, because my wife claims I have none, normally. I know she's only kidding.

I hope.

Inspired after listening to Penny's song played numerous times over the CD player in my office, I decided to put my artistic mixing talents to work. Jeff's songs deserved at least that much. I took them to the studio, and remixed not only his song for her, but an entire album worth of music from the band's rehearsal sessions. Mike liked them so much that he had them produced. And, wouldn't you know it, Penny's song is currently sitting in the top 20 of the nation's Rock'n'roll charts.

Patrick 'Murph' Murphy could add another 'collar' to his list of accomplishments, and Jake Rivers Private Investigative Services received a Gubernatorial Citation for civic duty, which I proudly display in my inner office.

I brought home a couple of raffle and lottery tickets, and gave the twins a preliminary example of the concept of 'chance' and the laws of probability, in explaining to them the term, "getting lucky." They seemed to have no problem grasping the concept. My wife, Nina, understood completely.

Special thanks to the following artists and companies for their contribution of free clip art.

Stockio.com

Johnny_Automatic

FreePNGimg.com

Clker.com

GOODFREEPHOTOS

IsaacGooggle

OnlyGFX.com

Image/s: Girl with Umbrella vintage public domain

PublicDomainPictures.net

FREE * SVG

Sun Line Art/Free Clipart Vectors

Openclipart/Nizips

Pixabay.com

Gordan Johnson

Noorataijala

BedexpStock

Mohamed Hassan

André.

About the author.

Joe Mannherz is a Physical Therapist by profession. Retired. He has been singing since the age of 8. From boy soprano in his church choir to tenor in his high school and later college chorus. He also plays several instruments. He's even built his own Vibraphone and Marimbas.

He has been a member of the Barbershop Harmony Society for over 45 years; a 30-year member of the Baltimore Symphony Chorus; a member of the Handel Choir and the Concert Artists of Maryland. He has been the Musical Director of Harford County's "Bay Country Gentlemen" and Harrisburg's "Keystone Capital Chorus". He is currently the Artistic/ Musical Director of his jazz quintet "High Five" and the "Baltimore Vocal Jazz Ensemble." Along with directing/music arranging/vocal coaching, he can add several stage appearances to his credit; A Funny thing happened on the way to the Forum, 1776, Man of La Mancha, Sound of Music, O'er the Ramparts, Little Mermaid, Jesus Christ Superstar, Beauty and the Beast and the Wizard of Oz to name a few of the most recent.

Made in the USA
Middletown, DE
02 November 2024

63729046R00076